Withdrawn

the
Quarreling
Book

the Quarreling Book

By Charlotte Zolotow

pictures by Arnold Lobel

HarperCollins*Publishers*

The Quarreling Book
Text copyright © 1963 by Charlotte Zolotow
Text copyright renewed 1991 by Charlotte Zolotow
Illustrations copyright © 1963 by Arnold Lobel
Illustrations copyright renewed 1991 by Adam Lobel
For information address HarperCollins Children's Books, a division
of HarperCollins Publishers, 10 East 53rd Street, New York,
NY 10022.

Library of Congress Catalog Card Number: 63-14445
ISBN 0-06-026975-8
ISBN 0-06-026976-6 (lib. bdg.)
ISBN 0-06-443034-0 (pbk.)

For Elizabeth Janeway

It was a rainy gray morning, and Mr. James forgot to kiss
Mrs. James good-bye when he left for the office.

Mrs. James felt quite cross because of this and because the rain made the day so gray. So when Jonathan James came down for breakfast, she was sharp with him.

"Oh, for goodness' sake!" she said. "Why did you wear that shirt again today? It's filthy!"

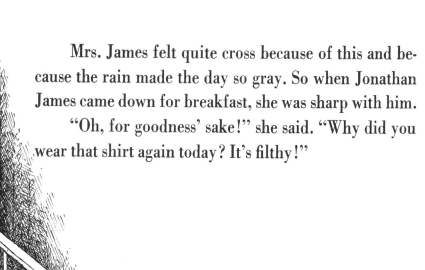

The shirt looked clean to Jonathan, and he thought her unfair. Because of this and because the rain made the day so gray, he turned on Sally James when she came down for breakfast.

"Can't you ever get down in time?" he said. "You'll be late to school for sure."

The clock said eight-fifteen, which was the time Sally was supposed to come down, and she thought Jonathan was completely unreasonable. Because of this and because the rain made the day so gray, when Sally got to school and met her best friend, Marjorie, in the hall, she looked at her and said, "Where'd you get that awful raincoat? It looks like a boy's."

Marjorie, who thought the raincoat was a beautiful shade of yellow, felt Sally was very unpleasant, and because of this and because the rain made the day so gray anyway, when she got home from school and found her little brother playing with her dolls she said, "Why do I have to have a little sissy for a brother?"

Eddie, her little brother, always played with her dolls and she had never minded before, and he thought her most unkind. Because of this and because he couldn't go outdoors to play in the rain, Eddie went to his room and shoved the dog off his bed, where the dog was sleeping.

But the dog didn't mind the rain. She thought Eddie was playing so she put her front paws down and her hindquarters up and her tail began wagging.

She pounced on Eddie and they rolled over and over wrestling together until the dog won and sat down on Eddie's chest and began licking his face.

This tickled and made him laugh, and he was laughing so hard that when Marjorie came in looking for a pencil for her arithmetic homework, he gave her his best one with a new eraser.

She was so grateful she couldn't help smiling and saying, "Thank you very much." She started out of the room and then turned back.

"You really aren't a sissy," she said.

She couldn't find the paper she'd copied the problems on, and she had to call up Sally to get them. She forgot she was mad at her.

"Hello, Sally?" she said, and she sounded so friendly that Sally was sorry she had said that about the raincoat. She gave Marjorie the homework and said, "It's really not so bad, that raincoat. You just have to get used to the color." Then she hung up feeling better and ran back upstairs, humming to herself.

She met Jonathan at the top of the staircase. "Hi, there, Johnny," she said. "I wasn't late at all." And she smiled at him so pleasantly that Jonathan said, "I was just teasing you."

"It's O.K.," said Sally.

Just then Mrs. James came into the hall. Jonathan said, "I'll put this in the laundry tonight for sure, Mom." And Mrs. James was so pleased that he remembered she said, "All right, dear. I couldn't have hung the wash in all this rain anyhow. Tomorrow will do as well."

Around five o'clock the sun came out. Everything
looked glistening and clean, and the birds began to sing

just as Mr. James came home and gave Mrs. James a great warm hello kiss before he went upstairs to wash for dinner.